W9-AHJ-657

On Eagles' Wings

and other things

To Ava — 1987
From —
Grandma Doris
& Grandpops Lee

THE JEWISH PUBLICATION SOCIETY
Philadelphia • New York • Jerusalem *5747–1987*

On Eagles' Wings
and other things

by Connie Colker Steiner

For the family that made my comings and goings possible,
Mark, Paul, Elisabeth, my parents, and Joel

I wish to acknowledge the unflagging support and encouragement of my editor, David Adler

Manufactured in the United States of America
Library of Congress Cataloging in Publication Data

Steiner, Connie.
On eagles' wings and other things.

Summary: After World War II children from various parts of the world arrive in Israel to make it their new home.
[1. Israel—Emigration and immigration—Fiction. 2. Emigraton and immigration—Fiction. 3. Jews—Israel—Fiction] I. Title.
PZ7.S826130n 1987 [E] 86–20147
ISBN 0–8276–0274–X

Designed by Adrianne Onderdonk Dudden

Avraham lived in the hills of Yemen.

Eli lived in Tunisia,
near a quiet sea.

Adena lived in America,
in a city full of traffic.

Mira lived in Poland, on a mountainside.

Avraham's house, in Yemen,
was made of mud and grass.
It had only one room.

Eli's family lived in one room
of a one-story house in Tunisia.
It had a dirt floor painted blue.

Adena's house, in America, had five rooms. Her parents kept green plants to remind them of the country. Adena kept shells to remind her of the seashore.

Mira's house, in Poland, had once been a hotel. She, and the other children who lived there, were orphans. Their parents had died during the terrible years of World War II.

In Yemen, Avraham's mother folded
her family's small wardrobe:
dresses, jackets, tunics, and trousers.

Avraham and his brothers gathered the *siddur,*
the *shofar,* and the Torah scroll.
Avraham's father prayed that they be granted a safe trip.

In Tunisia, Eli and
the smaller children
helped their parents pack.
They put clothing, linen,
and dishes into a big trunk.

They carefully wrapped
the family Hagaddah.

Into another trunk they put rice, beans,
coffee, tea, sugar, and dried peppers.

In America, Adena's apartment was nearly empty. Only the stove and the refrigerator remained.

Adena and her parents drove to the harbor. They watched men load their furniture, books, clothing, and dishes onto a big boat.

In Poland, Mira put a dress,
a nightgown, underwear,
and a warm sweater
into her knapsack.

She turned to help the younger children.
All the boys and girls and their grown-up
helpers were packing quickly.

Avraham lay on his mat.
He remembered the weeks of feast and celebration.
He dreamed of the great journey.

Adena crawled into
a sleeping bag.
She imagined her bed
on the big boat, sailing
across the ocean.

Eli slept near his brother
on a sheepskin blanket.
His parents slept
behind the hanging rug that
separated their bed from his.

Mira lay on her cot, too excited to sleep.

The sun rose in Yemen. Outside, Avraham found
a caravan of camels and donkeys and a crowd of people.

He was lifted onto a camel.
The journey began in song.
The caravan rode from village
to village, and more
people joined them.
Rough land, wild animals, and
highway robbers could not steal
joy and hope from the travelers.
After many days they reached
a village of tents. People who spoke
Hebrew welcomed the newcomers.

One day a great silver bird arrived.
Into the bird climbed Avraham and his family and neighbors. The bird soared into the sky.
Avraham's father was not surprised.
He laughed, "Is it not written that we will return to our land on the wings of eagles?"

The sun rose on the coast of Tunisia.
Eli and his family boarded a boat.
They waved good-by to friends and cousins.
"Someday we will come, too!" said the relatives.
The boat moved away. The figures on the shore
became small. Domes and minarets went by.

The trip took three days. The boat was crowded.
Near Eli, there were not just people, but animals,
too! Eli made friends with some horses.
In France, Eli and his family changed to a bigger,
finer boat. The passengers spoke many languages
but had one feeling: We are all coming home.

It was morning in America. Adena looked up at her apartment from the street.
She put her hand in her pocket and felt the shells she had saved from her collection.

At the airport, Adena and her parents boarded the plane.
They buckled their seat belts. Up they went.
They flew above the clouds and across the ocean.
Night came. No one slept. People walked in the aisles and talked.
Someone began to sing a Hebrew song. Others joined in.
Adena felt close to these strangers, who suddenly seemed part of her own family. Soon they would reach the land.

It was dawn in Poland.
The children formed two lines.
Each child had a partner.
Everyone squeezed into
the back of a covered truck.
Up and down they rumbled.

The truck stopped. The children climbed into
a train that took them over the border, out of Poland.
They were not safe yet, and Mira was afraid.

They continued west by train,
across the lands of Europe.

At last, the children reached France.
Mira rested and studied.
She even had time to learn the Hebrew alphabet.

One day a beautiful boat arrived to gather
the children who had come so far.
It sailed proudly, under the Star of David.

Avraham arrived in Israel.
He stumbled off the big bird
that was really an airplane.
His father knelt and kissed the earth.
Avraham knew he was far from Yemen.
Men and women wore strange clothing.
The land was different.

But above him waved his own blue and white flag. Smiling people said, "*Shalom, shalom!*" And the sound of a familiar prayer filled Avraham with joy: "Thank You, God, for allowing us to reach this day!"

Adena arrived in Israel. Down the airplane steps she scrambled. Then came her parents and the others who had come to Israel from America.

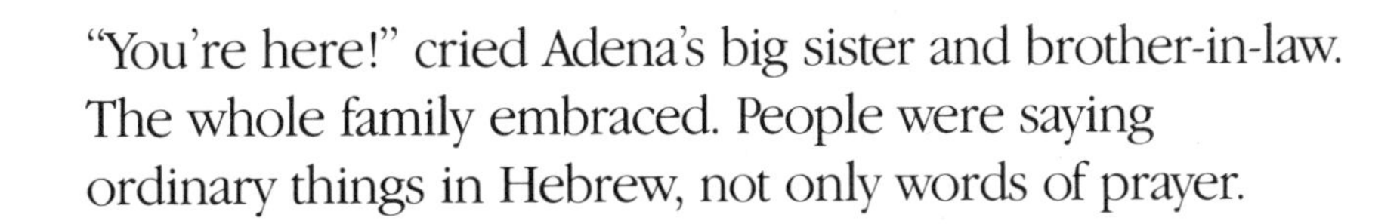

"You're here!" cried Adena's big sister and brother-in-law. The whole family embraced. People were saying ordinary things in Hebrew, not only words of prayer.

Adena scooped up some pebbles from the sandy ground. She put them in her pocket where they mingled with the shells from her old collection. It made her happy to think of them together.

Eli's boat reached Israel at night.
Everyone crowded on deck for a first look.
Beyond the port spread a city built upon the side of a mountain. The lights of the mountain were reflected in the sea and echoed in the sky.

Men wrapped themselves in prayer shawls
as the ship put down anchor. With dawn,
the city slowly awoke. Tunisia was part of long ago.
What would the real Israel be, they wondered.

Mira's boat reached Israel during the day.
The children pressed together at the railing.
Mira watched a tree-shaded city
rise above the harbor.

As the boat drew closer, she could clearly
see the men who worked on the docks.
The men waved and shouted, "*Baruch ha-ba!* Welcome!"
From nearby came the merry sound of an accordion.
Mira stepped onto solid, sun-baked land
and knew at once that she belonged.

Avraham, Adena, Eli, and Mira came to grow up in the new State of Israel. They brought with them dreams. Often they found that their new home was very different from the place they had imagined.

But it was home.

They joined Jews from around the world
who were coming to build the land.
What work there was to do!

Everyone knew he was needed
and—even better—wanted.

Afterword

The four children of the story represent the scattered Jews who came to Israel at the time of its rebirth.

Mira, of Poland, somehow survived the nightmare of Nazi Europe. For her and others, Israel was a chance to heal and begin life anew.

Eli is a Jew of Tunisia, in North Africa. He experienced no disaster comparable to the Holocaust. But Jews in the Moslem world were often oppressed and certainly did not enjoy equal rights with their Moslem neighbors.

Avraham is from Yemen, an isolated Moslem country in Asia. There, Jews maintained unique traditions and kept strong the love of Zion. When word came that there was a real Jewish state, nearly the entire Jewish population prepared to leave. They were airlifted to Israel as part of the famous project known as Operation Magic Carpet.

The little American, Adena, reminds us of the Western Jews who enjoyed freedom and prosperity. Some went to Israel because of their love and desire to build the Jewish homeland. They were few. Not all who made the trip stayed. We are guessing that Adena and her family forged new roots and became true Israelis.

Israel in 1948 was barely fledged and immediately went to war. It was a tiny country. The Jews who arrived there were not always well and strong. Yet Israel managed to absorb them and renew the Hebrew language as well. Between 1948 and 1952 the Jewish population of the land more than doubled.

The ingathering continues—with Soviet Jews, Ethiopian Jews, and the quiet, individual arrival of others.